Be Brave, Little Lion!

Ursel Scheffler

Be Brave, Little Lion!

ILLUSTRATED BY
Ruth Scholte van Mast

Translated by J. Alison James

North-South Books

NEW YORK · LONDON

Copyright © 2000 by Nord-Süd Verlag AG, Gossau Zürich, Switzerland
First published in Switzerland under the title *Pass auf, Lea Löwenkind!*
English translation copyright © 2000 by North-South Books Inc.
All rights reserved.
No part of this book may be reproduced or utilized in any form
or by any means, electronic or mechanical, including photocopying,
recording, or any information storage and retrieval system,
without permission in writing from the publisher.
First published in the United States, Great Britain, Canada,
Australia, and New Zealand in 2000 by North-South Books,
an imprint of Nord-Süd Verlag AG, Gossau Zürich, Switzerland.
Distributed in the United States by North-South Books Inc., New York.
Library of Congress Cataloging-in-Publication Data is available.
A CIP catalogue record for this book is available from The British Library.
ISBN 0-7358-1264-0 (TRADE BINDING)
1 3 5 7 9 TB 10 8 6 4 2
ISBN 0-7358-1265-9 (LIBRARY BINDING)
1 3 5 7 9 LB 10 8 6 4 2
Printed in Belgium
For more information about our books, and the authors and artists
who create them, visit our web site: www.northsouth.com

"Hey, you can't catch me!" cried Lea
to her brothers. Nimbly, she climbed out
on a ledge.

Joe and Jack chased after her.

With a great leap, Lea jumped across
the crevice.

"What's wrong? Aren't you coming?" called Lea.

Joe and Jack looked at each other. Lea was a much better jumper than they were.

"I don't feel like it," said Joe.

"It's cooler here in the shade," said Jack.
He lay down next to a sage bush and
closed his eyes.

Father Lion lay on the other side of the river under a large tree.

Lea looked over at him.

Father usually slept all day. Especially when he had eaten well—like last night.

Mother Lion lay with the other lionesses in front of the cave. They were sleeping, too.

Lea wasn't tired at all! Since nobody would play with her, she would go exploring by herself.

She jumped over stones and boulders.

What was that strange hill of sand?

Nervously Lea sniffed it. It didn't smell bad at all!

But suddenly her face was itching and tickling all over. Termites! Lea had poked her nose into a termite hill. She swiped the termites off her face with her paw. Then she ran on.

The little lion crossed the dry scrub land along the river bank. *Mmm.* Lea twitched her nose. What was that wonderful smell? Porcupine! There one was, sitting in the grass! Lea wanted to catch it.

Carefully, she crept behind the
porcupine. *Whoosh!* It disappeared into
its hole in the ground!

Lea stuck her nose into the hole very
slowly, because she knew that a bundle
of quills in the face would really hurt!

Suddenly, a hyena bounded up and
hissed, "Go away!"
Startled, Lea ran down to the river.

It was the end of the dry season, so
the river was only a tiny stream.

Lea dug herself a hole, just like Mother and Father Lion always did. It filled up with water.

Just as she was about to take a drink,
she heard a loud snort behind her.

A giant rhinoceros came crashing
through the bushes!

Lea had never seen a rhinoceros up close.

"Out of my way," puffed the rhino, and stomped past her.

"This is my water hole," protested Lea.

"Get out of here, or I'll trample you!" growled the rhinoceros.

Shocked, Lea jumped to the side. The rhinoceros drank and then made room for a baby rhino. It was just a few weeks old, and already it was bigger than Lea!

Lea raced back to her father. "Father," she panted, "that stupid rhinoceros just chased me away from my water hole."

"Were you scared?" asked Father Lion.

"A lion is never afraid. Not even of a rhinoceros. Running away is cowardly. Lions are brave. We fear no one."

"You're not afraid of *anyone?*" asked Lea.

"No, not anyone," claimed Father Lion, and proudly shook his mane. Then he laid his head down on his front paws and closed his eyes.

Lea ran to where Mother and the other
lionesses were resting. She told about her
adventure on the river.

"Run away when someone is stronger
than you," said Mother Lion. "That is the
wise thing to do."

The other lionesses nodded.

"But Father said that running away is cowardly," said Lea. "A lion must be brave and afraid of no one."

"It's fine to be brave when you are big and strong like your father. But you are just a small cub," said Mother Lion.

In the late afternoon, the sun still burned the dry land. There wasn't a cloud in the sky. "We need the rains to come soon," said Mother Lion.

As the sun dropped lower in the sky, the lions went down to the river. A herd of gazelles quickly ran away when they saw the lions. A pair of giraffes kept a respectful distance. And the hippopotamuses went the other way.

"You see, Lea, lions aren't afraid of anyone," said Father Lion. "Everyone is afraid of us."

They heard a thundering noise in the distance.

"Is the rainy season finally beginning?" asked Mother Lion, looking up at the cloudless sky.

Father Lion pricked up his ears and listened.

This thunder meant danger! He knew that it came from the hunters' deadly weapons.

"We must sleep in the cave," urged Father Lion. "Come!"

For the first time, Lea saw fear in his eyes.

"Why are we running away?" Lea asked Father Lion. "Are you afraid of the thunder? Thunder isn't dangerous. Thunder brings rain. That's what Mother said, anyway."

"That isn't thunder," said Father Lion. "It's the sound of guns."

During the night, the sky filled with clouds. Thunder crashed and banged, and lightning crackled. It was normal thunder.

The storm split open the clouds
and rain poured down on the dry land.
It rained for hours and hours.

"Thunder *does* bring rain!" cried Lea.
"Joe and Jack, come out of the cave!
Water is falling from the sky! Lots and
lots!"

Lea jumped around in the rain. She
sang and she danced.

Her brothers came out of the cave to join her.

"Water is wonderful!" cried Lea.

And then she jumped in a puddle so it splashed Joe and Jack.

They splashed her back.

Puddles were everywhere. Soon the
three lion cubs were rolling in the cool,
gooey mud.

Father Lion lay on a cliff and watched over them. He pricked up his ears. There it was again . . . that dangerous thundering in the distance.

He had to investigate. He had to find out where the hunters were, where they were going, and what they were planning to do.

While their father was gone, the cubs
played in the lake. The rain had filled it
up again. It was wonderful.

"When is Father coming back?" Lea asked that evening.

"Soon, I hope," said Mother Lion.

Father Lion didn't return until the next morning.

He was very worried. "We'll move to the mountains," he said.

"Why, Father?" cried Lea. "It is so pretty here."

Father lion looked at her for a long time. "I saw the hunters shoot a giant elephant," he said.

"Were you afraid?" asked Lea.

Father Lion was silent.

"Fear makes us cautious. And caution is not cowardly," Mother Lion replied. "Father is right. Be glad that he has made such a wise decision. Come, children."

So the lion pride set off across the plains to the mountains. When the sun turned red that evening, they reached the cave that Father Lion had found on his journey. Here they would be safe from the hunters.

Ursel Scheffler was born in Nuremberg, a German city where many toys are made. She has written more than one hundred children's books, which have been published in fifteen different languages. Her other easy-to-read books for North-South are *The Spy in the Attic; The Man with the Black Glove; Grandpa's Amazing Computer;* and a trio of adventures featuring a sly fox and a duck detective: *Rinaldo, the Sly Fox; The Return of Rinaldo, the Sly Fox;* and *Rinaldo on the Run.*

Ruth Scholte van Mast was born in Vreden, Germany. She drew a lot as a child, especially animals and children. She trained as a graphic artist, and drew printing patterns for wallpaper. She now works as a freelance children's book illustrator. Her first book for North-South, *Grandpa's Amazing Computer*, was also written by Ursel Scheffler.

Other North-South Easy-to-Read Books